ALL FALL DOWN

Written by Bill E. Neder
Illustrated by Liisa Chauncy Guida

HARCOURT BRACE & COMPANY

Orlando   Atlanta   Austin   Boston   San Francisco   Chicago   Dallas   New York
Toronto   London

The tigers climb up.

The bears climb up.

The clowns climb up.

The dogs climb up.

The monkey climbs up.

All fall down!